Clifford's BIG DICTIONARY

Based on the Scholastic book series "Clifford the Big Red Dog" by
Norman Bridwell

SCHOLASTIC INC.

New York   Toronto   London   Auckland
Sydney   Mexico City   New Delhi   Hong Kong

Produced by Downtown Bookworks Inc.

Cover design by Angela Navarra
Interior design by Georgia Rucker Design

Library of Congress Cataloging-in-Publication Data

Clifford's big dictionary.
     p. cm.
  "Based on the Scholastic book series Clifford the Big Red Dog: by Norman Bridwell Scholastic Inc. : New York, 2010."
  ISBN 978-0-545-21772-9 (hardcover)
 1. Picture dictionaries, English--Juvenile literature. 2. English language--Dictionaries--Juvenile literature. 3. Clifford (Fictitious character : Bridwell)--Juvenile literature. I. Bridwell, Norman. Clifford, the big red dog. II. Title.

PE1629.C584 2010
423'.17--dc22

2010022720

ISBN 978-0-545-21772-9

12 11 10 9 8 7 6 5 4 3 2   11 12 13 14 15

Printed in Singapore 46
First printing, September 2010

Clifford's BIG DICTIONARY

Table of Contents

🦴 How to Use This Book 🦴

A dictionary is a big book of words. **Clifford's Big Dictionary** uses pictures of Clifford, his friends, and other things to teach you words.

Some of the words in this book are words you know. Some of the words may be new to you. Every word in this book has a picture beneath it. The pictures can help you figure out what the words say if you can't read yet or if you are just learning to read.

The words in each section all begin with the same letter. The uppercase and lowercase version of that letter will appear with a very big Clifford at the beginning of the section.

The letters are in alphabetical order. A is first and then comes B, then C. Z is last. If you can sing the alphabet, you know the order of the letters. All of the letters in the alphabet are listed on the edge of the right-hand page. If you are in the B section, the B in the list on the edge of the page will be in a red bar. If you are in the P section, the P on the edge of the page will be in a red bar.

You can flip through the book and learn words. Or you can look up a word if you know what letter it begins with. For example, if you know that **car** begins with a C, you can find the C section by looking at the edge of the page for a C in the red bar.

The page numbers are on the bottom of every page.

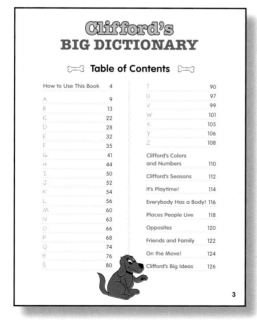

You can also turn to the Table of Contents to find out on which page the C words begin.

How to Use This Book

cake

This yummy **cake** has pink frosting.

Every word will be followed by a sentence using that word. This sentence, along with the picture, will help you understand what the word means. The word described in the picture will be bold and red.

Sometimes you will see a picture of a single thing. The word for that picture will appear above the picture.

Some of the pictures in this book show lots of different things. Those pictures will have a blue arrow pointing to the object described above it.

carrot

Carrots are crunchy. Bunnies and people like to eat them.

Some words have two different meanings. These words may have two different pictures and two different sentences explaining the word's meanings.

wave

Emily Elizabeth **waves** to someone she knows.

wave

Clifford swims in the ocean **waves**.

Now all you have to do is turn the page and learn some words!

Clifford and Emily Elizabeth like to read. Have fun reading with them!

above

The beach ball is **above** Emily Elizabeth's head.

acorn

Clifford finds an **acorn** in the grass.

act

Clifford can **act** like a fire engine.

afraid

Clifford is **afraid** of the jack-o'-lantern.

after

Charley slides down Clifford's back **after** Jetta.

airplane

This toy **airplane** can fly.

alien

An **alien** arrived in a spaceship!

almost

Cleo and T-Bone's sand castle is **almost** as big as Clifford.

a lot

Emily Elizabeth smiles **a lot**.

always

Clifford **always** helps his friends have fun.

anchor

An **anchor** is used to keep a boat from floating away.

animal

Dogs, bunnies, cats, and squirrels are all **animals**.

apple

Apples grow on trees.

around

Emily Elizabeth tries to wrap her arms **around** Clifford's nose.

artist

Emily Elizabeth likes to paint. She is an **artist**.

asleep

Clifford had a long day of playing and now he is **asleep**.

baby

When Clifford was a **baby**, he was a small red puppy.

back

Clifford is lying on his **back**.

backpack

A **backpack** can hold many things, like a book or a snack.

backward

Clifford is looking **backward** while he runs. Watch out, Clifford!

bag

The **bag** is full of Clifford's favorite snacks.

bake

Emily Elizabeth likes to **bake**. She made a cake!

ball

It's fun to throw, catch, kick, and bounce a **ball**.

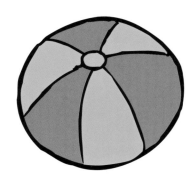

ballerina

Emily Elizabeth looks like a pretty **ballerina** in her tutu.

barn

Clifford and his pals are hiding around the **barn**.

baseball

A pitcher throws a **baseball** to a batter.

baseball bat

The batter hits the baseball with a **baseball bat**.

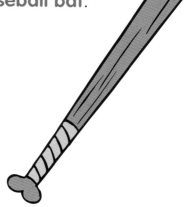

baseball glove

A **baseball glove** makes it easier to catch the ball.

basket

Clifford has a **basket** full of flowers.

basketball

Clifford helps out when the kids play **basketball**.

bat

Bats come out at night.

bath

Clifford takes a **bath** with his ducky.

beach

Clifford and Emily Elizabeth fly a kite at the **beach**.

bed

When Clifford was a puppy, he slept in this **bed**.

bee

The **bee** says "buzzzzzz."

before

Clifford will go down the slide **before** the boy.

beg

T-Bone **begs** for a treat.

behind

T-Bone is **behind** Clifford's paw.

bench

A **bench** is a nice place to sit in the park.

between

Clifford squeezes **between** Emily Elizabeth's feet.

bicycle

Clifford has an extra-big **bicycle**.

A a
B b
C c
D d
E e
F f
G g
H h
I i
J j
K k
L l
M m
N n
O o
P p
Q q
R r
S s
T t
U u
V v
W w
X x
Y y
Z z

big

Clifford is one **big** dog.

binoculars

Binoculars help you to see things that are far away.

bird

These **birds** live on Birdwell Island.

birthday

It's Emily Elizabeth's **birthday** and she's having a party!

bite

Someone took a **bite** of this dog bone.

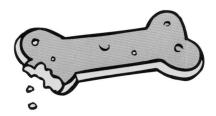

block

You can stack **blocks**.

blow

Clifford will **blow** out the candle on his cake.

bone

Dogs like to chew on **bones**.

book

It's lots of fun to read **books**!

boot

Boots keep your feet warm and dry when it is raining or snowing.

bounce

Emily Elizabeth likes to **bounce** the ball.

bow

T-Bone and Cleo tie a **bow** on Clifford's tail.

box

There are tasty dog treats in this **box**.

boy

Vaz, Charley, and Dan are all **boys**.

broom

A **broom** is used to sweep the floor.

brother

Zo is Flo's **brother**. They have the same mother and father.

bubble

There are lots of **bubbles** in Clifford's bath.

buried

Clifford is **buried** under the sand.

bus

Many children ride a **bus** to school.

butterfly

Here are one purple **butterfly** and one blue **butterfly**.

button

Mr. Miyori has three big **buttons** on his coat.

cake

This yummy **cake** has pink frosting.

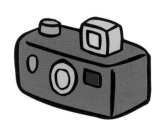

camera

A **camera** is used to take pictures.

candle

There is one **candle** on this birthday cake.

candy

Candy is sweet.

candy cane

Candy canes taste minty.

cap

This **cap** is much too big for Clifford.

cape

T-Bone is wearing a **cape** like a superhero.

car

This **car** is red, just like Clifford.

A a
B b
C c
D d
E e
F f
G g
H h
I i
J j
K k
L l
M m
N n
O o
P p
Q q
R r
S s
T t
U u
V v
W w
X x
Y y
Z z

carousel

A **carousel** spins round and round. This one has different animals to ride on.

carrot

Carrots are crunchy. Bunnies and people like to eat them.

cat

Cats have whiskers and long tails.

catch

Clifford will **catch** the ball.

cement mixer

A **cement mixer** is a truck that carries and pours cement.

chair

Emily Elizabeth likes to read in a comfortable **chair**.

chimney

Clifford sees Santa going into the **chimney**.

city

Clifford grew up in a **city** with lots of buildings.

Clifford

C is for **Clifford**!

climb

Clifford has to **climb** onto a toy truck to reach the dog bones.

cloud

Clouds are white or gray and come in lots of different shapes.

cold

This drink looks nice and **cold**.

costume

Emily Elizabeth is wearing a witch **costume**.

cousin

Rex is Clifford's **cousin**. He belongs to Emily Elizabeth's cousin Laura.

cover

T-Bone **covers** his eyes while his friends hide.

cozy

Clifford is **cozy** inside the warm mitten.

crab

Crabs crawl along the ocean floor.

crawl

Emily Elizabeth **crawls** on the floor looking for Clifford.

crayon

You can color pretty pictures with **crayons**.

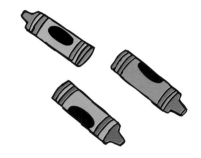

cry

Emily Elizabeth might **cry** if she is sad.

cupcake

This **cupcake** has vanilla frosting.

curl

Clifford likes to **curl** up for a nap.

cut

Scissors can **cut** paper.

A a
B b
C c
D d
E e
F f
G g
H h
I i
J j
K k
L l
M m
N n
O o
P p
Q q
R r
S s
T t
U u
V v
W w
X x
Y y
Z z

dad

Mr. Howard is
Emily Elizabeth's **dad**.

dance

Clifford likes to
dance when he
hears music.

dark

At night, it is **dark** outside.

daydream

Clifford **daydreams** about fun times in the park.

decorate

Clifford helps Emily Elizabeth **decorate** the Christmas tree.

different

These two balloons are **different** colors.

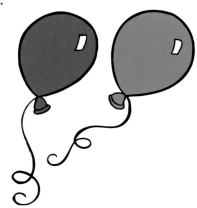

dig

Clifford helps to **dig** a deep hole.

dish

Clifford has one **dish** for food and one for water.

dive

T-Bone and Cleo **dive** into Clifford's dish for a swim.

dock

Clifford, Emily Elizabeth, and their friends go fishing on the **dock**.

dog

Clifford is the biggest, reddest **dog**.

doghouse

Clifford rests in his big **doghouse**.

dolphin

Dolphins like to jump out of the water.

door

You go into and out of the house through the **door**.

down

Clifford chases Emily Elizabeth **down** the hill.

drop

Emily Elizabeth **drops** one side of her jump rope.

A a
B b
C c
D d
E e
F f
G g
H h
I i
J j
K k
L l
M m
N n
O o
P p
Q q
R r
S s
T t
U u
V v
W w
X x
Y y
Z z

each

Each leaf is a different shape and color.

ear

Clifford has floppy **ears**.

earmuff

Clifford's **earmuffs** keep his ears warm.

eat

T-Bone loves to **eat** his bone.

elbow

Your arms bend at the **elbows**.

Emily Elizabeth

Emily Elizabeth is Clifford's best friend.

enjoy

Clifford **enjoys** a sunny day at the beach.

envelope

A letter is mailed in an **envelope**.

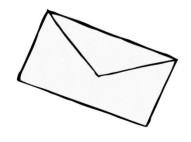

A a
B b
C c
D d
E e
F f
G g
H h
I i
J j
K k
L l
M m
N n
O o
P p
Q q
R r
S s
T t
U u
V v
W w
X x
Y y
Z z

33

every

Every egg in the Easter basket is beautiful.

excited

Cleo is so **excited**. She sees her friends coming and she can't wait to play with them!

exercise

Emily Elizabeth likes to **exercise**. She knows that moving her body is good for her.

eye

Clifford's **eyes** are wide open.

eyeglasses

Samuel wears **eyeglasses** to help him see.

fall

In the **fall** season, Clifford, Emily Elizabeth, and Charley play in the leaves.

fall

Clifford may **fall** down if he's not careful.

fast

Clifford makes the boat go really **fast**.

fat

Mrs. Sidarsky is one **fat** mouse.

feather

Norville the bird has blue **feathers**.

fence

A **fence** around a yard can keep a dog from running away.

ferry

The Birdwell Island **ferry** takes people over the water to Birdwell Island.

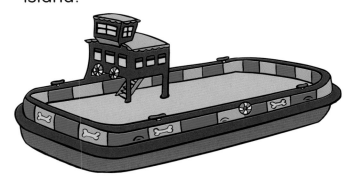

fetch

Emily Elizabeth throws a Frisbee, and Clifford runs to **fetch** it.

fill

Emily Elizabeth **fills** the bucket with sand.

firefighter

A **firefighter** helps to put out fires.

firehouse

The firefighters keep their trucks at the **firehouse**.

fire hydrant

Firefighters connect their hose to a **fire hydrant**. This gives them water for putting out fires.

fire truck

The **fire truck** sounds its siren as it races down the street.

A a
B b
C c
D d
E e
F f
G g
H h
I i
J j
K k
L l
M m
N n
O o
P p
Q q
R r
S s
T t
U u
V v
W w
X x
Y y
Z z

fish

Here are two **fish**: a gold one and a blue one.

fishing rod

You use a **fishing rod** to catch fish.

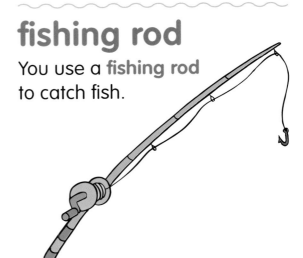

flag

This **flag** has a big dog bone on it.

flashlight

A **flashlight** helps you to see things in the dark.

float

Clifford can **float** on his back.

flower

Flowers grow in the spring when it's warm outside.

fly

Birds can **fly**.

follow

Clifford **follows** Emily Elizabeth when they skate.

food

People and animals eat different kinds of **food**.

football

It's fun to play catch with a **football**.

friend

Emily Elizabeth spends lots of time with her **friends** Jetta and Charley—and their dog **friends**.

A a
B b
C c
D d
E e
F f
G g
H h
I i
J j
K k
L l
M m
N n
O o
P p
Q q
R r
S s
T t
U u
V v
W w
X x
Y y
Z z

frightened

Cleo looks **frightened**. Something scared her.

Frisbee

Clifford can catch a **Frisbee** in his mouth.

frog

This **frog** is green.

fruit

Apples and pineapples are two kinds of **fruit**.

funny

Something very **funny** is making Clifford laugh.

fur

Clifford's **fur** is red.

A a
B b
C c
D d
E e
F f
G g
H h
I i
J j
K k
L l
M m
N n
O o
P p
Q q
R r
S s
T t
U u
V v
W w
X x
Y y
Z z

game

Clifford plays a **game** with Cleo and T-Bone.

gate

A **gate** lets you get from one side of a fence to the other.

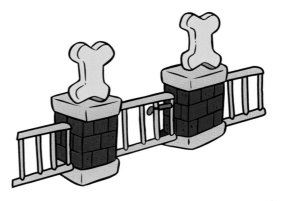

ghost

Here comes a big white **ghost**!

gift

It's nice to surprise your friends with **gifts** like these.

giggle

Emily Elizabeth **giggles** when Clifford does something funny.

girl

Jetta, cousin Laura, Mary, and Emily Elizabeth are all **girls**.

give

Emily Elizabeth **gives** Clifford a valentine.

goal

Clifford kicks the soccer ball toward the **goal**.

goggles

People wear **goggles** when they swim so they can see things underwater.

going

Clifford is **going** for a walk.

good

Emily Elizabeth is **good** at jumping rope.

good-bye

Emily Elizabeth waves **good-bye**.

grass

Grass is soft and green.

grow

Tiny puppies **grow** and **grow** and **grow** to be big dogs.

hamburger

Some kids like to put ketchup on a **hamburger**.

handle

You can pull a wagon by its **handle**. - - - - - -

handstand

Clifford is so strong, he can do a **handstand**.

hang

T-Bone had better **hang** on to Clifford's tail.

happy

Emily Elizabeth is **happy** when she's with Clifford.

hat

A **hat** can keep you warm or keep the sun out of your eyes.

heart

Here are one pink **heart** and one red **heart**.

helmet

It's important to wear a **helmet** when you ride your bicycle.

help

Clifford likes to **help**. Here, he **helps** the kids cross this river.

hide

Clifford tries to **hide** behind the tree. Do you see him?

high

Clifford is flying **high** in the sky.

high five

Charley and Emily Elizabeth give each other a **high five**.

hip

Emily Elizabeth spins the hula hoop around her **hips**.

hit

Clifford will **hit** the baseball with his bat.

hold

Clifford was such a small puppy, Emily Elizabeth could **hold** him in one hand.

hole

Clifford dug a very deep **hole**.

home

This doghouse is Clifford's **home**.

hop

Daffodil the bunny likes to **hop**.

horn

Blow a **horn** like this one to make music.

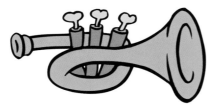

hose

Water comes out of a **hose**.

hot

This cocoa is **hot**.

hot dog

Here is a **hot dog** on a bun.

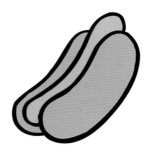

house

Some people live in a **house** like this one.

houseboat

Samuel lives in a **houseboat**, which is a house that floats on water.

howl

Clifford and his friends **howl** at the moon.

hug

Emily Elizabeth gives her big red dog a big **hug**.

hula hoop

Clifford keeps the **hula hoop** moving.

hungry

Clifford is so **hungry**, he can't wait to eat!

ice cream

There are so many delicious flavors of **ice cream**!

ice cream truck

Everyone is happy to see the **ice cream truck**.

ice-skate

Clifford and Emily Elizabeth **ice-skate** on the frozen pond.

idea

Clifford came up with a good **idea** for giving Emily Elizabeth a ride.

inside

Clifford is **inside** Emily Elizabeth's backpack.

instrument

Horns and drums are two kinds of musical **instruments**.

into

Somebody put dog treats **into** a treat bag.

introduce

Emily Elizabeth **introduces** her dog, Clifford.

A a
B b
C c
D d
E e
F f
G g
H h
I i
J j
K k
L l
M m
N n
O o
P p
Q q
R r
S s
T t
U u
V v
W w
X x
Y y
Z z

jack-o'-lantern

A **jack-o'-lantern** is a pumpkin with a face carved out of it.

jar

This **jar** holds Clifford's treats.

jewelry

Mrs. Bleakman likes to wear **jewelry**. She has a bracelet and earrings on.

join

Clifford's friends **join** him above the treetops. They can see a lot up there!

joke

Someone told Clifford a funny **joke**.

jump

Emily Elizabeth can **jump** really high.

jump rope

Clifford moves quickly when he skips with his **jump rope**.

kick

Emily Elizabeth can **kick** the ball really hard.

kid

Kids are smaller and younger than grown-ups.

kite

When it's windy you can fly a **kite**.

kitten

A **kitten** is a baby cat.

knee

Emily Elizabeth's socks go up to her **knees**.

kneel

Emily Elizabeth **kneels** to pet her tiny puppy.

knot

Jetta ties her sweater in a **knot** around her neck.

ladder

A **ladder** helps you to reach things that are high up.

ladybug

Ladybugs have little black spots.

lap

Emily Elizabeth is holding a book in her **lap**.

last

Mac is the **last** dog to dive into the water dish.

laugh

Clifford starts to **laugh** when his friends do something funny.

laundry

Clifford and his mouse friends play in the **laundry** basket.

lawn mower

A **lawn mower** cuts grass.

leaves

It's fun to jump in the **leaves** in the fall.

A a
B b
C c
D d
E e
F f
G g
H h
I i
J j
K k
L l
M m
N n
O o
P p
Q q
R r
S s
T t
U u
V v
W w
X x
Y y
Z z

letter

There are 26 **letters** in the alphabet!

lick

Clifford **licks** Emily Elizabeth.

life preserver

A **life preserver** can help people who have trouble swimming.

lighthouse

A **lighthouse** shines a light onto the sea so that sailors can find their way to land.

little

Birdy is a **little** yellow-and-blue bird.

long

This dog has **long** hair.

loud

Clifford can get pretty **loud** when he sings.

lunch box

You can bring your lunch to school in a **lunch box**.

love

Emily Elizabeth **loves** her big red dog.

A a
B b
C c
D d
E e
F f
G g
H h
I i
J j
K k
L l
M m
N n
O o
P p
Q q
R r
S s
T t
U u
V v
W w
X x
Y y
Z z

mail

It's fun to get **mail** from friends.

mailbox

To send a letter, put it in the **mailbox**.

mail truck

A **mail truck** delivers letters and packages.

many

There are **many** animals going down the slide.

map

A **map** is a picture of a place that shows you where everything is. This is a **map** of Birdwell Village.

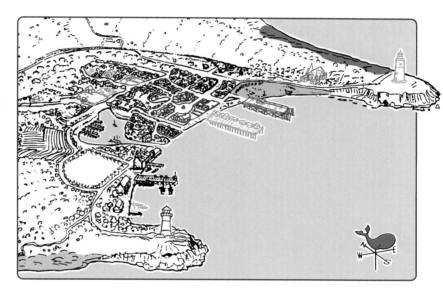

mask

Emily Elizabeth wears a **mask** that looks like Clifford.

mess

Clifford made a **mess** with the paint.

middle

Flo, Clifford, and Zo are sitting together. Clifford is in the **middle**.

mitten

Mittens keep your hands warm when it is cold outside.

mom

Mrs. Howard is Emily Elizabeth's **mom**.

moon

When the sun goes down, you can often see the **moon** in the night sky.

move

Clifford makes the sailboat **move**. He blows air into the sail.

music

You can make **music** with your voice or with an instrument.

A a
B b
C c
D d
E e
F f
G g
H h
I i
J j
K k
L l
M m
N n
O o
P p
Q q
R r
S s
T t
U u
V v
W w
X x
Y y
Z z

nap

Clifford curls up with his teddy bear for a **nap**.

nest

Birds live in a **nest**.

net

Emily Elizabeth catches fish in her fishing **net**.

never

Clifford would **never** be mean to his friends.

new

Look at the shiny **new** toy fire truck!

newspaper

You can read about things that are going on in the world in the **newspaper**.

next

It's Cleo's turn **next** to go down the waterslide.

next

The man and woman are sitting **next** to each other on the bench.

night

The dogs howl at the moon at **night**.

nobody

Nobody is sleeping in this bed.

nothing

There is **nothing** hanging on this hanger.

number

You count things with **numbers**.

123

A a
B b
C c
D d
E e
F f
G g
H h
I i
J j
K k
L l
M m
N n
O o
P p
Q q
R r
S s
T t
U u
V v
W w
X x
Y y
Z z

oar

An **oar** is used to paddle or move a rowboat.

ocean

Clifford plays in the **ocean** at the beach.

octopus

An **octopus** has eight tentacles that are like arms.

on

Clifford is sitting **on** the baseball glove.

open

The doggy door is **open**. Who's outside?

or

Lights can be turned on **or** off.

ouch

Ouch! A crab pinched T-Bone's nose. That hurts!

outside

Clifford and Emily Elizabeth like to play **outside**.

A a
B b
C c
D d
E e
F f
G g
H h
I i
J j
K k
L l
M m
N n
O o
P p
Q q
R r
S s
T t
U u
V v
W w
X x
Y y
Z z

pail

At the beach, you can fill a **pail** with sand.

paint

If you mix blue and yellow **paint**, you'll have green **paint**. Then you can **paint** a picture.

paintbrush

Use a **paintbrush** to paint a colorful picture.

paper

You can draw a picture on a piece of **paper**.

parade

Clifford, Emily Elizabeth, and Charley march in a **parade**.

party

Clifford is having fun at a **party**.

pedal

The bicycle has **pedals** for pumping.

pedal

Emily Elizabeth **pedals** her bicycle to make it go.

pencil

You can write letters or your name with a **pencil**.

pet

Emily Elizabeth **pets** her little puppy.

pickup truck

A **pickup truck** can carry big things like a sled or a bicycle.

picnic

The ants are enjoying Clifford's **picnic**.

picture

Emily Elizabeth paints a **picture** of her favorite dog.

pier

A **pier** is a big, long dock. This is the tourist **pier** on Birdwell Island.

pigeon

Pigeons are birds that live in cities.

play

Everyone likes to **play** with Clifford.

playful

Clifford is a **playful** puppy.

please

Clifford always says "**please**" when he asks for something.

pocket

Mr. Kibble has a comb and brush in his **pocket**.

point

Emily Elizabeth **points** at the butterfly.

A a
B b
C c
D d
E e
F f
G g
H h
I i
J j
K k
L l
M m
N n
O o
P p
Q q
R r
S s
T t
U u
V v
W w
X x
Y y
Z z

police car

The **police car** blasts its siren when it's rushing to get someplace.

poodle

Cleo is a purple **poodle**. A **poodle** is a kind of dog.

pool

Clifford and his friends go swimming in the **pool**.

popcorn

Popcorn is yummy and buttery.

post office

You can mail letters in a mailbox or at the **post office**.

present

Surprise! Emily Elizabeth has a **present** for somebody.

proud

T-Bone is **proud** because he won a medal.

pull

Clifford **pulls** the football by its lace.

pumpkin

Pumpkins are orange and round.

puppy

Clifford was a small red **puppy**.

push

The frog **pushes** T-Bone away.

A a
B b
C c
D d
E e
F f
G g
H h
I i
J j
K k
L l
M m
N n
O o
P p
Q q
R r
S s
T t
U u
V v
W w
X x
Y y
Z z

question

Emily Elizabeth has a **question**.
"Is anybody home?" she asks.

quick

Zo is one **quick** cat.

quiet

Clifford is being very **quiet**.
He's not making any noise.

quilt

There is a purple **quilt** on Emily Elizabeth's bed.

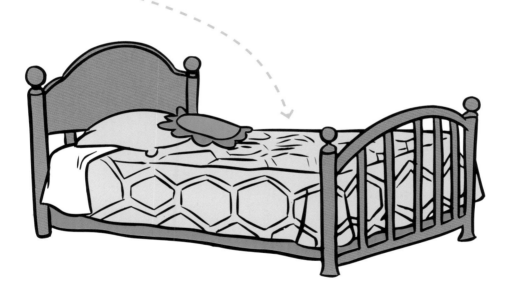

rabbit

Emily Elizabeth's first pet was a **rabbit** named Daffodil.

rake

In the fall, you can use a **rake** to move the leaves off of the lawn.

rain

Clifford keeps his friends dry in the **rain**.

rainbow

After it rains, look for a **rainbow** in the sky.

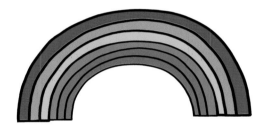

reach

Emily Elizabeth can just **reach** Clifford's nose.

read

Emily Elizabeth likes to **read** books.

ready

Emily Elizabeth is **ready** to hit the baseball.

relax

After a long day of playing, Clifford likes to **relax**.

restaurant

This **restaurant** serves fish. Other **restaurants** serve different kinds of food.

ribbon

Here are some green and red **ribbons**.

ride

Emily Elizabeth likes to **ride** on Clifford's back.

roll

Clifford and the ball **roll** on the ground.

roof

This house has a brown **roof**.

round

Balls are **round**.

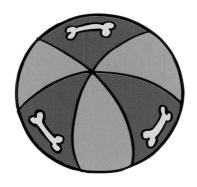

rowboat

Someone has to paddle a **rowboat** to move it around the water.

run

Run, Clifford, **run**!

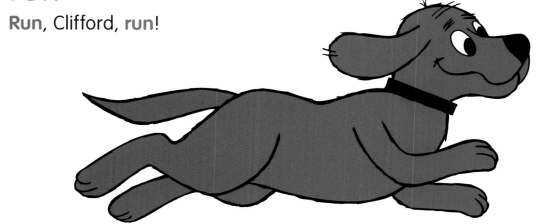

A a
B b
C c
D d
E e
F f
G g
H h
I i
J j
K k
L l
M m
N n
O o
P p
Q q
R r
S s
T t
U u
V v
W w
X x
Y y
Z z

sad

Emily Elizabeth feels **sad** when she misses Clifford.

sailboat

A **sailboat** captures the wind in its sail.

sand

There is plenty of **sand** at the beach.

sand castle

You can build a **sand castle** with some wet sand.

scarf

A **scarf** keeps your neck warm when it's cold out.

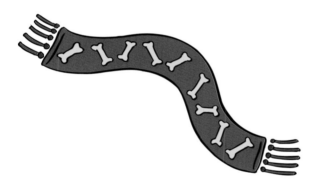

school

A **school** is where you learn new things.

score

Clifford **scores** a basket for his team.

seagull

Seagulls live near the water and like to eat fish.

A a
B b
C c
D d
E e
F f
G g
H h
I i
J j
K k
L l
M m
N n
O o
P p
Q q
R r
S s
T t
U u
V v
W w
X x
Y y
Z z

seal

Seals are good swimmers.

sea star

Sometimes a **sea star** will wash up on the beach.

seesaw

Friends can go on a **seesaw** together to make it go up and down.

shade

T-Bone and Cleo are under the **shade** of the umbrella.

shell

You can collect pretty **shells** like these on the beach.

shirt

Charley wears a striped **shirt**.

shoe

Shoes go on your feet.

shop

Different **shops** sell things like beach toys and kites.

shout

Emily Elizabeth **shouts** for Clifford to come for dinner.

shovel

You can dig in the sand or dirt with a **shovel**.

sign

This **sign** says that the bus stops here.

sing

Emily Elizabeth **sings** "Happy Birthday."

A a
B b
C c
D d
E e
F f
G g
H h
I i
J j
K k
L l
M m
N n
O o
P p
Q q
R r
S s
T t
U u
V v
W w
X x
Y y
Z z

sister

Flo is Zo's **sister**. They are in the same family.

sit

T-Bone **sits** on Clifford's paw.

ski

Clifford and Emily Elizabeth **ski** down the mountain.

skirt

Emily Elizabeth wears a black **skirt**.

sky

The **sky** is clear and blue.

sled

It's fun to ride on a **sled** in the snow.

sleep

It looks like Clifford has gone to **sleep**.

slide

Emily Elizabeth loves to go down the **slide**.

smile

Clifford's **smile** makes everyone happy.

snail

Snails live in a shell.

sniff

Clifford likes to **sniff**. It helps him to learn about things.

snowball

The **snowball** grows bigger and bigger as Emily Elizabeth pushes it through the snow.

snowflake

The **snowflakes** taste good!

soccer ball

Kids play soccer with a **soccer ball**.

spider

This **spider** is hanging by a thread.

spiderweb

A hardworking spider made this **spiderweb**.

spill

Oops! Somebody **spilled** the paint.

spin

Clifford **spins** the carousel.

spot

This dog has **spots** on her back.

squeeze

Emily Elizabeth gently **squeezes** her big red dog.

squirrel

Squirrels like to eat acorns.

stamp

You need to put a **stamp** on a letter before you mail it.

First Class

stand

Emily Elizabeth **stands** on two feet, and Clifford **stands** on four.

star

The **stars** twinkle in the night sky.

A a
B b
C c
D d
E e
F f
G g
H h
I i
J j
K k
L l
M m
N n
O o
P p
Q q
R r
S s
T t
U u
V v
W w
X x
Y y
Z z

stick

If Emily Elizabeth throws a **stick**, Clifford will fetch it.

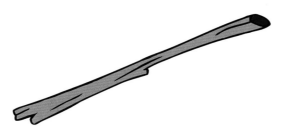

street

Emily Elizabeth's house is on this **street**.

string

Clifford holds on to the kite **string**.

stripes

Emily Elizabeth has pink-and-black **stripes** on her socks.

strong

Clifford is too **strong** for the other players to stop him.

sun

The **sun** is shining brightly.

surfing

Emily Elizabeth goes **surfing** when the waves are big.

swim

Clifford and Emily Elizabeth like to **swim** in the ocean.

swing

It's fun to ride on the **swings** at the playground.

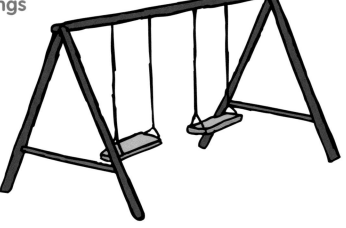

tail

Look out when Clifford wags his **tail**!

tall

This basketball player, Skyscraper Jackson, is very **tall**.

talk

Clifford **talks** to the fish.

tape

Clifford may have used a little too much **tape** on this present.

taste

Clifford tries to **taste** the ice cream truck!

taxi

In the city, people can ride in a **taxi** to get from place to place.

teacher

Miss Carrington is Emily Elizabeth's **teacher**.

teeth

Clifford's **teeth** are clean and white.

telescope

If you look through a **telescope**, you can see things that are far away, such as stars.

tennis racquet

You can hit a tennis ball with a **tennis racquet**.

tent

Emily Elizabeth sleeps in a **tent** when she goes camping with her family.

thinking

Emily Elizabeth is **thinking** about what she wants to do today.

through

Cleo jumps **through** the hoop.

throw

Clifford can **throw** the ball really far!

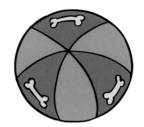

tiny

Clifford used to be a **tiny** little puppy.

tiptoe

Clifford quietly **tiptoes** away.

tired

It is almost Clifford's bedtime. He is **tired**.

together

Clifford and his friends are **together** a lot.

A a
B b
C c
D d
E e
F f
G g
H h
I i
J j
K k
L l
M m
N n
O o
P p
Q q
R r
S s
T t
U u
V v
W w
X x
Y y
Z z

tongue

"Aaah." When Clifford opens his mouth, you can see his **tongue**.

too

This collar is **too** big for the tiny puppy.

tool

You can build and fix things with these **tools**.

top

Clifford is on **top** of his friends.

towel

You can dry off with a **towel** after you go swimming.

toy

It's fun to play with **toys** like dolls, blocks, and **toy** boats.

toy chest

Clifford keeps his toys in a **toy chest**.

CLIFFORD'S PUPPY TOYS

tractor

A **tractor** is used on a farm.

traffic light

When the **traffic light** is red, it means "stop."

train

People can take a **train** from one place to another.

train tracks

Trains move along **train tracks**.

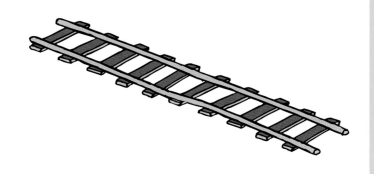

trash can

Garbage gets thrown into the **trash can**.

tree

This **tree** has many green leaves.

truck

This big red **truck** can hold a lot of dog food!

tunnel

If you're small, you can crawl through the **tunnel**.

turtle

A **turtle** has a hard shell.

uh-oh

"**Uh-oh.**" Emily Elizabeth looks worried about something.

umbrella

An **umbrella** keeps you dry when it's raining.

under

The bird is **under** the bench.

up

Cleo and T-Bone are floating **up**, **up**, and away!

upside down

Clifford is turned **upside down**!

use

Clifford tries to **use** the remote control.

A a
B b
C c
D d
E e
F f
G g
H h
I i
J j
K k
L l
M m
N n
O o
P p
Q q
R r
S s
T t
V v
W w
X x
Y y
Z z

valentine

It's nice to make **valentine** cards on **Valentine's** Day.

vegetable

Carrots, broccoli, and lettuce are all **vegetables**.

very

Clifford is **very**, **very** big.

veterinarian

Dr. Dihn is a **veterinarian**, or animal doctor.

wag

When Cleo is excited, she **wags** her tail.

wagon

You can fill a **wagon** with lots of different things like toys or balls.

101

wait

Clifford will **wait** to eat until his lunch is ready.

walk

Clifford is taking a **walk**.

wash

Emily Elizabeth **washes** Clifford with soap and water.

watch

Mrs. Handover wears a **watch** so she'll know what time it is.

wave

Emily Elizabeth **waves** to someone she knows.

wave

Clifford swims in the ocean **waves**.

wet

After he takes a bath, Clifford is all **wet**.

whale

Whales are the biggest creatures in the ocean!

wheelchair

Mary uses a **wheelchair** to help her get around.

whisper

Emily Elizabeth **whispers** a secret into Clifford's ear.

wind

The **wind** blows leaves all around Clifford.

window

Look out the **window** to see what the weather is like.

A a
B b
C c
D d
E e
F f
G g
H h
I i
J j
K k
L l
M m
N n
O o
P p
Q q
R r
S s
T t
U u
V v
W w
X x
Y y
Z z

wonder

T-Bone **wonders** what happened to his bone.

work

Emily Elizabeth **works** on her homework.

worried

T-Bone looks **worried**. He can't find his friends.

wreath

Clifford is wearing a **wreath** around his neck.

write

Clifford can **write** his name.

xylophone

Emily Elizabeth can make pretty music on a **xylophone**.

yard

Cleo's **yard** has fun things to climb and play on.

yay

"**Yay**!" Clifford and Emily Elizabeth are going on a fun trip.

yelp

Before puppies can bark, they give a little **yelp**.

you

You are reading this book. Clifford hopes **you** like it!

young

When Clifford was **young**, he was very small.

yummy

Clifford thinks hot dogs are really **yummy**.

zigzag

The car is driving in a **zigzag** path.

zipper

Mr. Howard's shirt
has a **zipper**.

zoom

Clifford and his friends **zoom** down the hill on their roller skates.

Clifford's Colors and Numbers

Can you count all of the colorful things with Clifford?

red fire truck

orange pumpkins

yellow balloons

green trees

blue birds

 purple candies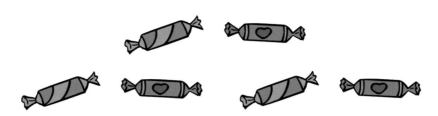

 pink shells

 black paw prints

 brown bones

 colorful butterflies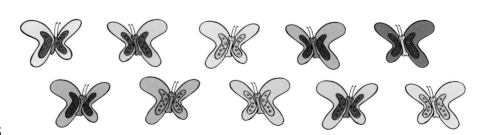

Clifford's Seasons

Clifford has fun all year long.

Winter

Christmas

Valentine's Day

Be my BiG ReD Valentine!

Spring

Easter

Summer

Fourth of July

Fall

Halloween

Thanksgiving

113

It's Playtime!

Clifford and Emily Elizabeth enjoy doing so many things. What do you like to do?

Baking

Playing Basketball

Camping

Fishing

Playing Football

Playing Hide-and-Seek

Spinning
Hula Hoops

Painting

Ice-skating

Reading

Skiing

Swimming

Playing
Soccer

People, animals, and fish all have different body parts.

Fur

Ear

Eye

Nose

Tail

Belly

Paws

Eye
Hair
Eyebrow
Nose
Fingers
Arm
Mouth
Leg
Knee
Feet

Claws

Shell

Fins
Tail
Scales

Wing
Beak
Webbed
Feet

Places People Live

People (and animals!) live in many different places.

Birdwell Island is an **island**. It is surrounded by water.

Cities have lots of buildings and people.

The **desert** is very dry.

Towns or **villages** have places to shop, work, and eat.

In the **country**, there is plenty of nature and open space.

People can live in a **house**, an **apartment**, or even a **houseboat**. Clifford has his own **doghouse**.

Opposites

Things that are completely different from one another can be called opposites. Here are some opposites.

Big red dog  **Small red dog**

Hot  **Cold**

Empty  **Full**

Awake 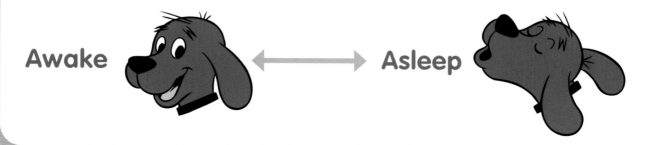 **Asleep**

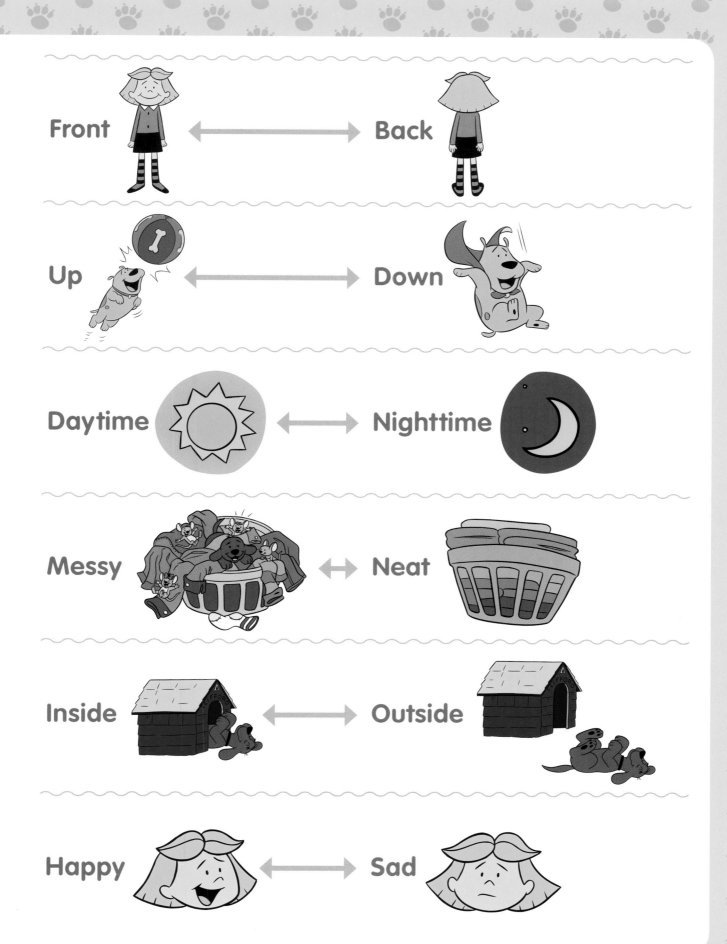

Front ⟷ Back

Up ⟷ Down

Daytime ⟷ Nighttime

Messy ⟷ Neat

Inside ⟷ Outside

Happy ⟷ Sad

Friends and Family

Mrs. Howard is Emily Elizabeth's **mom**.
Mr. Howard is Emily Elizabeth's **dad**.
Emily Elizabeth is their **daughter**.

Mrs. Howard is Laura's **aunt**.
And Mr. Howard is Laura's **uncle**.

Laura is Emily Elizabeth's **cousin**.

Charley and Jetta are
Emily Elizabeth's **friends**.

Clifford is Emily Elizabeth's **pet**. He is also her **friend**.

Zo and Flo are **brother** and **sister**. They have the same **mom** and **dad**.

T-Bone and Cleo are Clifford's **friends**.

On the Move!

There are many different ways to get around.

People ride in **cars** to get from place to place.

A **cement mixer** carries cement.

A **fire truck** brings firefighters to a fire.

A **truck** can move big things like furniture from one place to another.

A **mail truck** delivers letters and packages.

A **school bus** takes children to school and back home.

Police officers drive a **police car**.

A **tractor** is used on a farm.

Boats ride on the water.

A **rowboat** must be paddled.

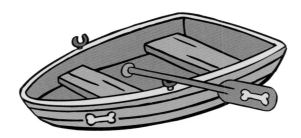

A **sailboat** is moved by the wind blowing into its sails.

A **ferry boat** carries people back and forth over the water.

It only takes a little to BE BIG!™

Share. If you have a toy and you let your friend play with your toy, you are **sharing**.

BE BIG and share by giving your friend one of your cookies or treats.

• • • • • • • • • • • • • • • • • • • •

Play Fair. **Playing fair** means following rules and taking turns when you play with your friends and classmates.

BE BIG and **play fair** by making sure everybody is included when you play tag or dress-up or duck-duck-goose.

• • • • • • • • • • • • • • • • • • • •

Have Respect. **Having respect** means you listen to other people's ideas, even if they are different from your own.

BE BIG and **have respect** by listening to your parents, even if they ask you to clean up your room or do something else you may not want to do.

Work Together. When you cooperate with your friends, family, or classmates, you are **working together**.

BE BIG and **work together** by building a block building with your friends.

Be Responsible. Being responsible means getting things done when people ask you.

BE BIG and **be responsible** by washing your hands before you eat dinner, cleaning up after yourself, and getting your work done on time.

Be Truthful. If you are honest and you don't lie, you are **being truthful**.

BE BIG and **be truthful** by telling the real story—even if you've eaten a sweet when you weren't allowed to, or if you've spilled something.

Be Kind. Be friendly and helpful to other people. That's **being kind**, and everybody likes a thoughtful, kind person.

BE BIG and **be kind** by saying "please" and "thank you," and by doing nice things for other people.

Believe in Yourself. If you are brave and try new things, you will learn to **believe in yourself** because you'll see that you can be really good at things if you practice.

BE BIG and **believe in yourself** by trying something brand-new — like ice-skating, or riding a bicycle, drawing a picture of yourself, or baking a cake.

• •

Be a Good Friend. To **be a good friend**, you must be helpful and kind to the people you care about.

BE BIG and **be a good friend** by being a good listener, by helping a friend who needs help, or by saying and doing things that will make your friends happy.

• •

Help Others. If someone needs help with something, like clearing the table, or putting away toys, you should help out. That's how you can **help others**.

BE BIG and **help others** by doing what they ask you to do right away, or asking them if they need your help.